I AM READING

MOOSE
and MOUSE

Written and illustrated by
COLIN WEST

KINGFISHER

To Cathie

KINGFISHER
An imprint of Kingfisher Publications Plc
New Penderel House, 283-288 High Holborn
London WC1V 7HZ
www.kingfisherpub.com

First published by Kingfisher 2004
This edition published by Kingfisher 2008
2 4 6 8 10 9 7 5 3 1

Text and illustrations copyright © Colin West 2004

The moral right of the author and illustrator has been asserted.

A CIP catalogue record for this book
is available from the British Library.

ISBN 978 0 7534 1640 2

Printed in China
1TR/1007/WKT/(SCHOY)/115MA

Contents

Mouse's Poem

Moose and Mouse were friends.

Moose was big
and strong.

But Mouse was the
one with brains.

Moose liked the outdoor life.

Mouse preferred
life indoors. He
made up poems on
his old typewriter.

One sunny day, Moose called on his friend Mouse.
There was a spring in his step as he walked up Mouse's path.

"Coming fishing?" asked Moose.

"Too busy!" said Mouse.

"I'm working on a poem."

Moose left Mouse to his typing.

Moose wandered down to the riverbank.

He found his favourite rock and sat down.

He fished in the river all morning.

Moose caught three big ones!

"*Just the thing for lunch,*" thought
Moose as he fried the three fish.
And they were delicious!

Moose wondered what his friend was
doing for lunch.
"*Maybe he's too busy to make
anything,*" he thought.

"*I know Mouse likes fish,*"
Moose thought.
So he made up
a bag of leftovers
for his friend.

Then he picked some lovely nuts and
berries to go with them.

Moose took the bundle to Mouse's house.

He tapped on the window.

"Hello, Mouse!" he cried.

"I've got a surprise for you."

Mouse frowned.

He didn't look up from his typewriter.

Moose tapped on the window again.

"Yoo-hoo!" he shouted.

"I've brought you some lunch!"

"I'm too busy to stop!" snapped Mouse.

"I'm working on my poem."

"I'll leave your lunch on the doorstep,"

said Moose.

"OK!" said Mouse rather crossly.

As Moose was about to leave, he noticed

Mouse's garden was looking a mess.

There were rotten apples all over the lawn.

"*Maybe Mouse is too busy to tidy up,*"

thought Moose.

Moose decided to help out.

He worked hard, picking up the rotten
fruit and putting it in an old sack.

It took him over an hour to finish.

Moose looked in
Mouse's window.
Mouse was still
at his typewriter.
Moose tapped
gently on the glass.

"Hello, Mouse," he said softly.
"I've tidied up your garden for you."

"Fine!" snapped Mouse.
"I'll see you
tomorrow!"
he added
rather rudely.

"Goodbye, then," said Moose.

Moose left the sack by Mouse's door.
He gathered up his things and wandered
home to bed.

Next day, Moose went to Mouse's house.

He noticed something odd.

The lunch bag was still on the doorstep.

But the sack of rotten apples was

missing!

Moose knocked on Mouse's door.

After a while it opened.

"Come in," said Mouse weakly.

se looked ill.

ou've been working too hard," said
Moose. Mouse nodded.
"But at least I've finished the poem,"
he muttered.

He showed it to Moose:

Moose is brave,
Moose is strong,
Moose works hard
All day long.

Moose is broad,
Moose is tall,
Moose is my
Best friend of all.

Moose is helpful
As can be,
And he's almost
As smart as me!

"Wow! You're so clever," said Moose,

beaming with pride.

"Maybe so, but I've got dreadful tummy ache," said Mouse sadly.
"I think it was that lunch you left me yesterday!"

The End

The Camping Trip

Moose was excited.
At last Mouse had agreed
to go camping with him.

Mouse told Moose all the things
to pack.
Mouse was good
at remembering
things.

"Thanks for being so helpful,"
said Moose.
He put everything in his backpack and
they were off.

Mouse wasn't too keen on camping.

He preferred home comforts.

"I hope the weather holds," he said as they left home.

They walked down the track towards
the woods.

"I hope there
aren't any
bears here!"
said Mouse.

"And I hope there
aren't any wolves
either!" he added.

Moose admired the view by the lake.

"How wonderful!" he sighed.

"Humph!" muttered Mouse.

"I've got a better view on my own wall – a picture of the Bahamas."

They walked into the woods.

"What a lovely sound!" said Moose as he
heard a woodpecker.

"Humph!" said Mouse.

"I prefer listening to a good tune on
my CD player!"

They reached a clearing at the top
of a hill and stopped for a while.
Moose breathed in deeply.
"What nice fresh air!" he said.
"If you ask me it's rather chilly,"
said Mouse.
"I prefer sitting indoors."

31

They walked and talked some more.
They watched the sun go down over
the hills.

"It's beautiful," said Moose.

"It's getting dark," observed Mouse.

"We should think about setting up
camp," announced Mouse.
"Let's look at the map and find a
good spot."

Moose was happy to follow Mouse.
Mouse was the clever one, after all.
Mouse led Moose through the woods.

By now it was very dark.

"It's a good job you reminded me to

bring the torch," said Moose.

They walked for a long while —
beside the lake, through the woods,
over a bridge and along a track.

"This looks like a good spot," said Mouse.

Moose nodded in agreement.

Mouse was good at finding places.

Moose unpacked their things.

Mouse told Moose how to put up
the tent.

It was quite hard work, but Mouse was
good at giving instructions.

"I'm glad you know how to do it!"
said Moose.

Before long, Moose and Mouse were in their sleeping bags.

Mouse took the torch and crept out of the tent.

Mouse seemed to know exactly where he was. And this wasn't surprising – he was in his own back garden!

Mouse let himself in.

He climbed into his own comfy bed.

That night, Mouse slept as soundly as ever.

And Moose slept like a log in his
sleeping bag.

In the morning Mouse woke up to the
smell of cooking.

"*That's funny,*" he thought.

Mouse was surprised to find Moose
making breakfast.

"M...m...morning, Moose," said Mouse.

"Morning, Mouse," said Moose.

"It's amazing how we ended up in your
back garden!"

"Y... y... yes," murmured Mouse.

"In fact," said Moose, "I'd almost think you did it on purpose!"

And they both chuckled as Moose served up breakfast.

The End

About the Author and Illustrator

Colin West has created over fifty children's books since leaving the Royal College of Art in 1975. He enjoys both writing stories and drawing pictures, so has published poetry books, story books and picture books. Colin wrote the *Monty the Dog* series, which was made into a cartoon for BBC television. He also has his own website, www.colinwest.com. Colin likes the differences between the two friends, Moose and Mouse, but admits, "I'm definitely more like Mouse – I like making up poems, listening to music and leaving the really hard work to someone else!"

Tips for Beginner Readers

1. Think about the cover and the title of the book. What do you think it will be about? While you are reading, think about what might happen next and why.

2. As you read, ask yourself if what you're reading makes sense. If it doesn't, try rereading or look at the pictures for clues.

3. If there is a word that you do not know, look carefully at the letters, sounds, and word parts that you do know. Blend the sounds to read the word. Is this a word you know? Does it make sense in the sentence?

4. Think about the characters, where the story takes place, and the problems the characters in the story faced. What are the important ideas in the beginning, middle and end of the story?

5. Ask yourself questions like:
Did you like the story?
Why or why not?
How did the author make it fun to read?
How well did you understand it?

Maybe you can understand the story better if you read it again!